"Stop, Amber, you're dazzling us!" Pearl gasped.

Lily and Pearl blinked. When they opened their eyes, a faint cloud of glitter hung in the air – but Amber was gone!

"Where am I?" Amber asked.

She sat on a cold floor in a damp basement.

"This isn't my house. Where am I?"

Amber stood up and straightened her red frilled skirt. It was dusty and torn. Her feet were bare.

"What is this? Is it a kitchen?" she wondered out loud.

There were rows of pans on a shelf, a bare wooden table and a big, open fireplace. The fire had burned low in the grate.

No fridge, Amber noticed. And no microwave. No food either, except for a large orange pumpkin on the table.

"I don't get it," Amber said out loud. "One minute I'm putting on a red skirt and twirling in my basement. The next thing I know I'm in a cellar in a big, old house!

"Where am I?" she said again.

But no one answered. No one at all.

2

Carefully, Amber went up the cellar stairs and turned the door handle. It was locked.

She sat on the top step, working out what to do next. *Maybe there's another door somewhere*, she thought.

So she went down again and searched in dark corners, opening a tall cupboard and trying not to squeal when a white mouse scuttled out.

"Cobwebs!" she muttered, brushing them from her arm. "Spiders. Mice!" And it was cold, here in the dark cellar. The fire had turned to ashes and Amber was beginning to shiver.

At last she ran up the stone steps again.

This time she rattled the door. "Let me out!" she cried. "You can't keep me locked in here, whoever you are. I want to come out!"

"You hear that, Louisa? She wants to come out!" a voice shrieked from the far side of the door.

Amber rattled the handle again. At last someone was coming to rescue her.

"She wants to come out!" a second voice echoed. "Well, Charlotte, shall we let her?"

"Not a chance!" Charlotte cried. "If we let her out she'll only put her grubby fingers on my silk dress. She'll smear the silver plates with her filthy hands!"

"Hey!" Amber cried. "Less of the grubby fingers and filthy hands stuff, OK!"

But when she looked at her hands, she saw that they were covered in soot. *How did that get there?* she wondered.

"So shall we open the door and beat her instead?" Louisa demanded.

"Good idea!" Charlotte agreed.

Beat me at what? At first, Amber didn't understand.

"Yes, let's beat her and punish her for being a lazy little misery!" Louisa could hardly wait to unbolt the door.

"You've got to catch me first!" Amber sprang back as the door was flung open. She saw two girls – one short, one tall – blocking her way.

Skinny Charlotte was dressed from head to toe in purple. Dumpy Louisa wore bright orange.

"There she is, the little nuisance!" Charlotte yelled, squeezing her wide purple skirt through the door.

"Catch her, beat her!" Louisa chanted.

Amber fled down the steps and dodged them both. She ran round the table and seized a sweeping brush. "Stay back!" she warned, holding it like a sword.

"Little misery!" Charlotte cried, darting at Amber. "Don't you dare defy me!"

"Useless girl!" Louisa raged, closing in.

Amber jabbed at Louisa with the brush. She wouldn't give in easily.

But there were two of them and only one of her. Soon Louisa and Charlotte had cornered Amber by the fireplace.

"Grab her!" Louisa roared.

"Pinch her. Squeeze her!" Charlotte cried.

The bullies came at her like a purple and orange storm, hands grabbing, slapping and tugging.

So Amber thrust the brush into the grate and raked through the ashes. She scooped them towards Charlotte and Louisa, raising a thick cloud of dust.

"Oh, you devil!" Charlotte cried,

coughing and covering her face.

"Little demon!" Louisa shrieked and choked.

Quickly Amber threw down the brush and dodged the two staggering girls. She dashed up the cold stone stairs, out of the dark kitchen, into the light.

3

"Help!" Amber cried.

Her voice echoed through the empty house.

She ran from room to room, each one grander than the one before. She fled along a hall with white marble floors and big gold mirrors.

"Help!" she shouted out from the tall windows.

She ran into a room lined with books, with a wide desk and a white-haired man quietly reading.

The old man looked up from his book and smiled.

"Help me!" Amber gasped. "Charlotte and Louisa are after me."

Taking earplugs from his ears, the man beckoned her. "Come, Cindy, and sit by me," he said kindly. "I won't let them harm you."

Cindy? Had she heard right? Nervously she stepped forward.

"Ah, Cindy, my dear," the old man sighed with a shake of his head. "I'm afraid your new sisters do not use you well."

"I'm not Cindy, I'm Amber. I don't have any sisters!"

"I have made many mistakes in my life," the old man said, ignoring Amber's protest. "But, my darling child, the greatest of all has been to marry again."

"I'm not your . . ." Amber began.

But just then footsteps came trampling down the hall and the library door flew open. A red-faced woman charged ahead of Charlotte and Louisa into the room.

"Aha, Cinderella, I knew we should find you here!" the woman shrieked.

Amber stared at her, then down at her own bare feet and ragged red skirt. *Cindy. Cinderella! The cold, dark cellar, the white mouse and the pumpkin . . . wow!*

Louisa and Charlotte stood behind their mother, covered in grey dust.

"She's wicked!" Louisa whined.

20

"She threw ash in my face!" Charlotte whimpered.

I stepped into a dream! Amber thought. *I'm living in a fairy tale!*

"I'm not wicked!" She spoke out firmly. "They were the ones who wanted to beat me and pinch me."

"No more than you deserve, you horrid girl," her stepmother shouted. She was tall and thin. She wore a blonde wig and too much make-up. "Husband, don't just sit there. Hand the girl over to me at once."

Amber stayed by the old man's side.

"Octavia, my dear," the old man protested mildy. "I'm sure that Cinderella meant no harm."

"I have ash in my mouth and in my eyes!" Charlotte pouted.

22

"It tastes horrid!" Louisa sniffled. Tears streaked her face.

"They flew at me in a rage," Amber explained. "It was two against one."

The old man blinked behind his small silver spectacles. "Perhaps, my dear, it would be better if you said sorry to your sisters."

But Amber held up her head. "I have nothing to say sorry for. They kept me locked up in the cellar and then they attacked me."

At this, Octavia seized her by the wrist and shook her. "Bad girl, have you no shame? You have ruined Louisa and Charlotte's beautiful dresses!"

"She must wash out every stain!" Louisa cried. "I don't care if her hands grow red

23

and sore, and her back aches."

"She must iron every crease and flounce up every frill!" Charlotte said. "Even if she stays up till midnight to get it done."

"Well, husband?" Octavia demanded.

The old man said nothing but lowered his head. His shoulders sagged as he let his wife take Amber away.

Sighing, he put in his earplugs and went back to his book.

"Miss Goody-goody – we know you're Father's favourite," Charlotte sneered.

From a high window looking down on to the cellar, she and Louisa watched Amber boil water in a huge black kettle over the open fire.

"This is *so* not fair!" Amber muttered to

herself. Octavia had locked the door and taken away the key.

"Here!" Charlotte pushed her purple dress through the window and let it fall on to the cellar floor.

"Scrub, scrub, scrub!" Louisa crowed as she flung down her orange gown.

Amber glared up at them. "Just you wait!"

"Oh-ho, little vixen!" Louisa mocked.

"Watch her –

she bites!" Charlotte laughed.

They vanished from the window and Amber heard their silly, chattering voices grow faint as they flounced off along the hall.

No way am I washing their rubbish clothes! she vowed to herself. She picked up the frilly dresses with their lace collars and wide, gathered skirts. *Octavia can do what she likes to me – I am not really Cinderella, I'm Amber. And I am not doing their tacky laundry!*

As she dumped the dresses on the table, Amber heard a clink of metal from the folds of Louisa's orange skirt. She found the pocket and quickly slipped her fingers inside, drawing out a big key.

"Hey!" she muttered. "I bet this key fits

the cellar door. Stupid Louisa forgot that
she left it there!"

Quick as a flash Amber darted up the
stone steps and tried the key. Sure enough,
it turned in the lock.

Freedom! Amber's heart beat fast as she
flung open the door. Daylight flooded the
long hall.

"That's it – I'm out of here!" Amber

muttered, setting off at a run.

She fled in her bare feet down the hall, past the mirrors and doors, until she came to some wide steps and double doors beyond.

Bump-bump went Amber's heart.

Behind her a door opened and Charlotte and Louisa stepped into the hall. "Cinderella is running away!" they screamed. "Catch her. Do not let her escape!"

Amber gasped then jumped down the five wide steps in one go. She tugged at a carved silver handle to open the wide doors.

"Grab her!" the girls screamed.

"Got you!" A broad-shouldered servant in a green velvet jacket grabbed her.

"Let me go!" Amber cried.

But Tom the footman carried Amber kicking and screaming back inside the house.

4

In the kitchen, washing and scrubbing the stains from the Uglies' dresses, Amber tried not to cry.

"When you've finished the washing, begin sweeping the floor," Octavia ordered. "And when you've done that, iron these petticoats. Don't go to bed until they're done."

Rub, *rub*. "I never knew that being

Cinderella was so miserable!" Amber sighed.

Scrub-scrub, rub-rub. She hung Charlotte's purple dress on a hanger and left it to drip.

Then she dunked Louisa's orange frock into the soapy water and began again.

"'Rub-a-dub-dub, three men in a tub!'" The cellar door opened and a boy appeared, whistling and chanting.

Amber stopped scrubbing.

"'Who do you think they be?'" The boy wore a grey jacket buttoned up to his chin. "'The butcher, the baker, the candlestick-maker . . .'" He came jauntily down the steps carrying a pair of big black boots. "'. . . Throw them out, knaves all three!'"

With that, he threw the boots on the table and opened up the tall cupboard.

"Hey!" Amber said with a glint in her eye. "Do you have the key to this dump?"

The boy shook his head. "The missus opened the door for me and locked it again behind me."

"The missus?" Amber asked.

"Her ladyship. Mrs Octavia, who ain't no lady, but thinks she's very high and mighty, believe me!"

"Ah!" Amber's hopes sank. "So who are you?" she asked.

The boy grinned. "Don't give me that, Cinders. You know who I am. I'm Buttons – the boy who cleans the boots around here. I call in twice a week with my spit and polish."

"And she always locks you in?" Amber checked.

"Just like you, Cinders," the boy nodded. "Only they keep you down here all the time, which ain't a nice life for no one, I don't suppose."

"I don't want to stay here," Amber confessed. "I want to escape."

The boot boy looked serious. "Hush!" he warned. "These walls have ears. Besides, you'd break your old dad's heart if you ran away."

Amber frowned. "He didn't exactly stick up for me back there," she pointed out.

Buttons sighed. "Look, since we're both in the same boat for the afternoon, I brought you a nice treat. Close your eyes and hold out your hand."

Wiping her hands on her tattered skirt, Amber did as she was told. When she opened her eyes she saw that the boy had placed a paper bag full of white sugar-mice in her palm.

"I got six of them. There, I thought they would cheer you up a bit!" Grinning, Buttons set to work on the dirty boots. *Spit – polish. Spit – polish.* "'Rub-a-dub-dub, three men in a tub!'"

"Thanks. I'll save them for later," Amber said quietly, just as the door opened and one of the Uglies appeared.

"Cinderella, we need you!" Louisa announced.

"Now!" Charlotte pushed Louisa to one side.

"I'm busy," Amber told them.

"We'll tell on you if you don't come straight away," Louisa yelled down the cellar steps.

"'. . . The butcher, the baker, the candlestick-maker!'" Buttons said with a wink.

"'Throw them out, knaves all three!'"

5

"Shall I wear my hair up or down for dinner tonight?" Charlotte asked. She sat in front of her bedroom mirror, fiddling with her curls.

"Who cares?" Louisa scoffed. "However you wear it, there'll be no boys to admire you!"

"Cinderella, fetch my curling tongs," Charlotte ordered. "Stupid girl, where did you put my hairbrush?"

"Cinderella, I need you to fasten the hooks on my dress." Louisa stamped her foot. "Now. Not in a month, you lazy thing!"

Amber pulled at Louisa's hooks until the tight blue dress was fastened.

"I've decided to wear the pink one instead," Louisa said, staring into the mirror. "Unhook me!"

Dress me. Undress me. Curl me. Straighten me. Tweeze my eyebrows. Tie my bows. Make me beautiful.

"Fat chance!" Amber said under her breath. She really was at the end of her tether with these two.

And their mother was worse.

Octavia swept into Charlotte's room

holding a white and silver card. "Oh girls!" she cried, ignoring Amber. "Our dream has come true."

"What is it, Ma?" Charlotte asked. She was in a bad mood because her hair wouldn't sit right.

Louisa wasn't happy with the bow at the waistband of her pink dress. "You tied it wrong!" she snapped at Amber.

Octavia waved the card in front of their faces. "It's an invitation."

"To what? Another boring tea party with lots of old people?" Louisa grumbled.

"Let me guess – a visit to Great-aunt Olive's house in the country," Charlotte muttered.

"Wrong. Wrong!" their mother cooed. "I shall read it out to you. Are you ready?"

"Go ahead," Charlotte and Louisa said with wide yawns.

Octavia cleared her throat. "'By Royal Invitation,'" she began.

The Uglies sat up straight and stared.

"'His Highness, Prince Charming, invites you to a Grand Ball at the Palace on Saturday . . .'"

"A Grand Ball!" Louisa let her mouth drop open.

"At the Palace!" Charlotte gasped.

Amber shook her head in disgust. *Yeah well, we all know what happens there*, she thought. *Big party. Handsome prince. Prince meets Cinderella. Prince dances with Cinderella . . . whoa!*

"Isn't it wonderful?" Octavia's smile split her face from ear to ear. "Girls – you know that Prince Charming is the most handsome man in the world!"

"I need a new dress!" Louisa said straight away.

"And shoes, stockings, ribbons, and definitely a new tiara!" Charlotte added.

"You shall have all of them," their mother promised.

And what I need to do, Amber thought, *is to get out of here – fast!*

Wash and iron, scrub and sweep. There were three days until the Grand Ball, and for the first day Amber worked from dawn till dusk.

"It's so not fair!" she muttered over and over.

On the second day, Octavia still guarded the key to the cellar and piled extra work on Amber.

Meanwhile, Charlotte and Louisa lounged around the house with cream on their faces and curlers in their hair. Busy pampering, they would send Amber to answer the many knocks on the door.

"Parcel for Miss Louisa and Miss

Charlotte!" the dressmaker told Amber. "It holds one peach-pink silk ball gown with puff sleeves and one ball gown in lilac, with a Bo-Peep bodice."

Five minutes later, the glove-maker arrived. "Two pairs of the finest white kid gloves for the young ladies," he announced.

Wearily, Amber carried the parcels upstairs.

Then the shoemaker appeared at the door, with shiny party shoes specially made to fit Miss Louisa and Miss Charlotte. "Size seven, wide fitting, and size nine narrow," he reported.

Finally, the jeweller came with two sparkling tiaras in blue velvet boxes.

The vain girls seized their new jewels

and tried them on, twirling and turning in front of their mirrors.

"My tiara sparkles more than yours!" Charlotte declared.

"But my peach-pink gown is more gorgeous by far!" Louisa answered back.

Amber shook her head. Didn't they know how stupid they looked in their puffed-up silk skirts and lace sleeves, with their tiaras on crooked and face-cream slapped on their cheeks?

That's it! Amber thought after a whole day answering the door. Being worked to death in the cellar was bad enough without sticking around to see the Uglies make fools of themselves on Saturday night. Besides which, there was the whole Cinderella–Prince Charming

thing that was about to kick off.

I'm definitely out of here! she thought. *The first chance I get!*

So, when the door knocker went *rat-a-tat-tat* for the tenth time that afternoon, and Amber ran to answer it, she already had a plan.

"Ribbons for Miss Charlotte," the boy at the door said.

Amber glanced at Tom the footman standing by the door. Then she opened the parcel. "These ribbons are purple," she said with a frown.

"That's what was ordered," the boy told her.

He was ready for a quick getaway, but Amber held him back. She made sure that

Tom was listening. "Miss Charlotte changed her mind. She wants pale green ribbons. And she wants them now, not in a month!"

The boy shrugged. "I've got more errands to run."

"Leave them with me. I'll do it!" Amber said. "It'll only take five minutes."

Tom took a step forward as if to stop her.

"Listen, you know what Miss Charlotte is like," Amber muttered to her fellow slave. "She'll scream and cry if she gets the wrong ribbons."

The footman raised his eyebrows then nodded. "OK, but be quick," he warned.

Amber ran down the wide street. She took the first turning then stopped. Her plan had worked. She was free.

No more Uglies, she thought. *No more washing and ironing for those airheads!*

But which way should she go now?

Looking around, Amber saw that the side street was narrow and led to more streets lined with shops. There was a butcher's and a baker's, a shop selling ladies' hats and one where men sat reading newspapers and drinking coffee.

"OK, which way?" Amber said out loud.

She turned again, into a bustling street full of stalls piled high with apples, carrots and cabbages.

Too crowded, Amber thought. She turned back. Then back again.

I'm lost, she thought. *I haven't a clue where I am, or which way I'm heading!*

49

A man pushed an empty cart along the
cobbled street. A woman stared at Amber
from behind her apple stall.

"In fact," Amber said out loud with a

sudden gasp, "I'm more than lost. I mean, here I am, stuck in a dream world. And I don't know how I arrived. Worse still, I haven't a clue how to get out!"

51

6

Dazed, Amber wandered down the street in her ragged red skirt.

The street curved round a bend. There were tall houses on either side and Amber didn't realise that she had walked full circle until she came back on to the wide main street, not a dozen paces from her own front door.

Loud voices roused her from her misery.

"Idiot!" a high voice screeched.

Amber looked up and saw Louisa, still wearing her crooked tiara and face-cream, tug angrily at the gold braid on their footman's coat.

"You were a fool to let Cinderella out of your sight!" Charlotte joined in. She pulled off Tom's white wig and stamped on it.

"Simpleton! Dunderhead!" Louisa piled on the insults.

"Cinderella tricked me," Tom mumbled. "She said she would change Miss Charlotte's purple ribbons for green."

"Green!" Charlotte shrieked, stamping her foot again and shaking out her curlers. "I wouldn't be seen dead in green ribbons at the Prince's Ball!"

Just then, sharp-eyed Louisa caught sight of Amber. "There she is!" she cried, darting down the street towards her.

Oh no! Amber turned and fled. She ran up a steep side street, up steps until she came to a dead end. Quickly she doubled back and slipped into the entrance to a boot maker's shop.

Charlotte and Louisa followed, shrieking and screaming. "Stop her! Trip her! Don't let her get away!"

They panted up the steps, stopped for breath then set off again.

Amber cowered in the doorway. So far the Uglies hadn't spotted her. But then she heard voices inside the shop.

"Thank you, Your Majesty," the boot maker said. "Your new boots will certainly

be ready in time for the Grand Ball."

"*Your Majesty?*" *Oh no, what have I got myself into now?* Amber wondered.

"Thank you, Master Beckett," a man's voice replied. "I will send my man to collect them tomorrow morning."

Louisa and Charlotte drew level as the door opened. Two men strode out – one all in plain black, the other handsome and dressed in a fine plum-coloured jacket, white trousers and high black boots.

Amber pressed against the wall. *Prince Charming in the flesh!*

Louisa and Charlotte gasped and grew pale under their face-cream. As they bowed their heads and curtsied low, Amber slipped quietly into the dark shop.

"Your Majesty!" Charlotte whispered, all a flutter.

"Miss Louisa and Miss Charlotte Osborne, at the Prince's service!" Louisa simpered.

The Prince couldn't help staring at their crooked tiaras, slapped-on face-cream and half-curled hair. "Enchanted," he said with a polite smile.

Amber watched silently while Louisa

uttons followed with a whistle and
rin.

"So do you want to hide at my place?"
offered. "It's round the corner, down
s alleyway."

Amber swallowed her pride and
dded. What else could she do?

"Get a move on and follow me," he
dered, leading her to a run-down house
th broken windows and a creaking
or. "It ain't much," he confessed. "But
s home!"

60

and Charlotte almost fainted with delight.

Meanwhile, the handsome prince bowed and strode on.

The boot maker's shop was piled high with boxes of nails, pieces of leather and hammers of all sizes. Amber sank down on a stack of sheepskin. But before she had time to rest, a voice she knew rang out.

"'Three blind mice, see how they run!'"

Amber jumped up. "Buttons, is that you?"

"'They all run after the farmer's wife!'" With a wide grin, the boot boy stepped out of a back room. "'Cut off their tails with a carving knife!'"

"What are you doing here?" she cried.

"What are *you* doing here?" he echoed.

"Running away. What does it look like?

Now answer my question."

"I'm bringing boots to be   a leaned against the counter,   fingers and humming his t   he you need a place to hide?"   th

Amber nodded quickly.   going back to that cellar!'   no

"Buttons, you've got to help

Just then, the boot make   o into his shop and spied her.   w Buttons. "I see you've got a   d And a pretty one too."   it

"'Did you ever see such a t   life . . .'" Buttons winked bac

"I'm out of here!" Amber   before the boot maker cou   more. *Ding-a-ling* went the   slammed the door.

7

Amber and Buttons got safely inside the old house just in time.

Out in the main street, voices shouted for Cinderella.

"Look for her down that alleyway," someone cried, and footsteps came running.

"She can't have gone far!" Octavia's voice shrieked. "Carry on searching.

Whatever you do, don't let her escape."

Inside the house, Amber shuddered.

"Wait here!" Buttons whispered. He stepped out into the alleyway and disappeared.

Can I trust him? What if he sneaks off and betrays me? Amber wondered. *Maybe Octavia will offer him a reward.* Trembling, she hid in a dark corner and waited.

After five minutes, Buttons returned, hands in pockets and whistling a new nursery rhyme. "That should do it!" he announced.

"What did you tell them?" Amber crept from the corner and peered out of the broken window. The alleyway was deserted.

"I stopped her ladyship and said I'd seen

and Charlotte almost fainted with delight. Meanwhile, the handsome prince bowed and strode on.

The boot maker's shop was piled high with boxes of nails, pieces of leather and hammers of all sizes. Amber sank down on a stack of sheepskin. But before she had time to rest, a voice she knew rang out.

"'Three blind mice, see how they run!'"

Amber jumped up. "Buttons, is that you?"

"'They all run after the farmer's wife!'" With a wide grin, the boot boy stepped out of a back room. "'Cut off their tails with a carving knife!'"

"What are you doing here?" she cried.

"What are *you* doing here?" he echoed.

"Running away. What does it look like?

Now answer my question."

"I'm bringing boots to be mended." He leaned against the counter, drumming his fingers and humming his tune. "I expect you need a place to hide?"

Amber nodded quickly. "I'm never going back to that cellar!" she vowed. "Buttons, you've got to help me!"

Just then, the boot maker came back into his shop and spied her. He winked at Buttons. "I see you've got a new girl, eh? And a pretty one too."

"'Did you ever see such a thing in your life . . .'" Buttons winked back.

"I'm out of here!" Amber left quickly before the boot maker could say any more. *Ding-a-ling* went the bell as she slammed the door.

Buttons followed with a whistle and a grin.

"So do you want to hide at my place?" he offered. "It's round the corner, down this alleyway."

Amber swallowed her pride and nodded. What else could she do?

"Get a move on and follow me," he ordered, leading her to a run-down house with broken windows and a creaking door. "It ain't much," he confessed. "But it's home!"

7

Amber and Buttons got safely inside the old house just in time.

Out in the main street, voices shouted for Cinderella.

"Look for her down that alleyway," someone cried, and footsteps came running.

"She can't have gone far!" Octavia's voice shrieked. "Carry on searching.

Whatever you do, don't let her escape."

Inside the house, Amber shuddered.

"Wait here!" Buttons whispered. He stepped out into the alleyway and disappeared.

Can I trust him? What if he sneaks off and betrays me? Amber wondered. *Maybe Octavia will offer him a reward.* Trembling, she hid in a dark corner and waited.

After five minutes, Buttons returned, hands in pockets and whistling a new nursery rhyme. "That should do it!" he announced.

"What did you tell them?" Amber crept from the corner and peered out of the broken window. The alleyway was deserted.

"I stopped her ladyship and said I'd seen

you scoot up the steps towards the Prince's Palace. She gave me a slap for my pains and told me I should have nabbed you and dragged you back home."

"Home!" Amber groaned. Home for her was a nice house with a nice garden and a dressing-up box in the basement – not that cobwebby cellar! "If only you knew!" she sighed.

Buttons shot her a quick look. "Anyhow, that should throw them off the trail. Come upstairs and meet my gran."

"Your gran?" Amber was surprised.

"Yeah. You didn't think I lived here all alone, did you?" Leading her upstairs, Buttons took her into a room with a warm fire and an old lady sitting in a rocking chair beside it.

"Cosy!" Amber murmured, looking round at the small table covered with a neat cloth, and a patchwork quilt on the bed in the corner.

"Gran, meet Cinderella!" Buttons announced. "She's run away from home!"

"Sshh!" Amber gasped. "Don't tell everyone!"

"Don't worry, she's deaf as a post," he grinned back, going up to the old lady and patting her hand. "Ain't you, Gran?"

She smiled and nodded back, then noticed Amber. "Who's this?" she croaked.

"A friend of mine!" Buttons shouted in her ear. "We're going to give her a cup of tea and take good care of her, ain't we, Gran?"

The old lady kept on nodding. "Come close to the fire," she said to Amber. "You must be catching your death of cold with your poor bare feet!"

Buttons made tea from a kettle boiling on the hob. "You're braver than you look,

65

Cinders," he said chattily. "I'll say that for you."

"Give the girl two spoons of sugar," his gran said from her rocking chair. "Looks like she needs them."

"What do you mean?" Amber asked him. "What's so brave about running away from that nuthouse?"

"Ah, you don't know her ladyship as well as I do," Buttons explained. "Before she married your dad she got through three husbands without even blinking!"

"No!" Amber gasped. "What happened? Did they all die?"

Buttons nodded and leaned forward. "None of them lasted. Once they marry her, the game's up. They either die of a heart attack, or who knows what else!"

Amber's eyes widened and her mouth fell open.

"Your old dad didn't know what he let himself in for with her ladyship," Buttons went on. "Three husbands dead already! The woman's a menace."

Amber frowned. "But Octavia doesn't like me. I'm in her way. So she'll soon call off the search party."

Buttons shook his head. "Like I said, you don't know her. She'll be after you like a hound after a fox, and when she finds you, she'll shake you to pieces!"

"Don't!" Amber gasped.

"Without even blinking," Buttons insisted. "She's a monster. And you know why she's so thrilled about the invitation to the Grand Ball, don't you?"

Amber shook her head.

"Because she wants to get those two ugly daughters of hers married and off her hands as quick as possible. And the best place to find a rich husband for them is at the Palace this Saturday."

"Right!" Amber got the point. "Lots of lords and counts and things will be there."

"And the Prince," Buttons reminded her.

"Remember, her ladyship will stop at nothing. If she gets one of those girls married off to the highest in the land, she'll think she's finally arrived!"

"You mean, she wants Louisa or Charlotte to marry Prince Charming?" Amber said with a frown.

"She longs for it," Buttons assured her. "She plans and schemes for it."

Amber sat back on her stool and thought for a while. "Well," she said at last, giving him a sad, quiet smile. "Don't worry about that."

"What do you mean?" Buttons asked, shooting her another sharp look.

Amber folded her hands on her lap. "I mean, Charlotte and Louisa are not going to marry Prince Charming, however much their wicked mum wants it."

"How do you know?"

"I just do," she insisted. "Trust me – it's never going to happen!"

As the time for the Ball drew near and every person in that crowded city held their breath ready for the big day, Amber sat with Buttons' grandmother.

"Don't go out!" Buttons ordered Amber as he left on an errand. "The minute you pop your head out of that door, someone will nab you and take you kicking and screaming back home!"

Home. That word again.

Amber sat by the fire, daydreaming about lounging in front of the TV with her mum and dad, or eating pizza with Lily and Pearl. *What are they doing now?* she wondered. *I bet they're going crazy, looking for me, calling my name and wondering where I am!*

"Can you sing me a nursery rhyme?" Buttons' gran asked suddenly in her cracked voice.

Amber shook her head.

"My boy, Buttons, sings me lovely rhymes," the old lady sighed. There was a pause, then she said, "Can you dance? I used to love to dance when I was your age."

Amber smiled and took pity on her. "I can dance a bit. Like this."

She stood up and tried a skipping step across the room.

"Pretty!" the old lady cried. "Now, something else!"

A twirl, Amber thought. She began to turn. Her red skirt flared out as she spun.

"More!" came the plea.

Spinning. Skirt flashing red. This was how it started! Amber turned on the spot.

Perhaps, if I do it again, faster and faster –

I can step out of the dream!

Amber twirled as fast as she could. She grew dizzy and sat on the floor, her eyes closed.

When she opened them again, the old lady was sitting in her chair by the fire, smiling and clapping her hands.

8

"Maybe I'm stuck here for ever!" Amber groaned. "Really and truly, I might never go home!"

So I stay here and marry Prince Charming, she thought. *Look on the bright side – to some people, being Cinderella is like winning the lottery!*

"Still here!" Buttons noted as he came back in through the door. He seemed less cheerful than when he'd gone out. There were no rhymes, smiles or wisecracks.

"Where else would I be?" Amber asked glumly. "I was just keeping your gran happy – dancing for her."

"That's nice," Buttons mumbled. He dumped two pairs of boots down on the floor. "The whole town's talking about the Ball. If you ask me, it's a lot of fuss over nothing."

"What happened to you?" Amber asked, rousing herself from her own misery. "Why are you in such a bad mood?"

"I'm not."

"Yes, you are. You're in a 'Here comes a chopper to chop off your head' mood."

"Oranges and flipping lemons," Buttons muttered, sitting on a stool and starting to clean the boots.

"Look me in the eye," Amber insisted. "Something's wrong, isn't it?"

"Yes, the world's gone mad over a party at the Palace. Everyone wants their boots cleaned and I only have one pair of hands, don't I? Carriages crammed with guests are blocking the streets. Ladies are hanging from windows crying that their wig makers have ruined their wigs!"

"It's not that," Amber said. "All that stuff's funny. Why are you sad?"

At last Buttons looked up from his polishing. "If you must know, I bumped into Tom the footman from your place."

"Are they still looking for me?"

Buttons nodded and brushed. "But I saw Tom and he told me some news. And what he said has brought this black cloud over my head."

"Which is?" Amber asked impatiently.

Brush-brush. "Which is what I don't want to talk about."

Amber snatched the boot brush from his hand. "Tell me!" she insisted.

Buttons sighed and looked straight into her eyes. "Tom says it's happened the way I feared it would – your running away has hit the old man very hard."

"The old man – my father?" Amber didn't know what else to call him.

"Yes, your old dad. Tom says his heart is breaking. He won't eat, he won't drink or sleep. Tom can see him fading fast."

"But he won't die just because I left!"

77

Amber cried. "People don't die of broken hearts."

"Ah, but they do when it's their only natural daughter," Buttons sighed. "It does strike at the heart of a man. And I'm only telling you what Tom said to me."

Taking a deep breath, Amber went over to the window. She looked down on the dark alleyway, heard rainwater dripping from the rooftops, saw puddles glint in the half-light. "That's terrible," she breathed.

"Life's hard," Buttons admitted. Then he waited.

Amber recalled the old man in his library – the rapid look of love on his face when he glanced up from his book and saw her.

She made up her mind on the spot.

"Where are you going?" Buttons asked

as Amber opened the door and headed down the stairs.

"To see my father," she replied.

Outside in the alleyway, the rain poured down.

"But if the missus gets her hands on you, she'll punish!" Buttons protested.

"You know what she's like."

Amber ignored him and walked on through the puddles. "Tell your gran thanks for the tea," she called to him over her shoulder.

9

Tom the footman opened Amber's grand prison door and let her in. "Your father's in his library," he told her quietly.

Amber trod along the wide marble hall, up the curving staircase. Her hair was dripping wet, her feet were covered in mud. At the door of the library she paused to look along the empty gallery. Then she knocked.

There was no answer, so she turned the handle and entered.

Her father was bent over a book, his hand across his face. He looked old and feeble.

Amber went towards him, gathering the courage to speak. "Father."

He glanced up, his face lined with sorrow. But when he saw Amber, that old look of love lit up his features. "Cinderella!" he whispered through happy tears.

"I'm home," she murmured, hearing rapid footsteps in the corridor, feeling her heart beat fast.

"More starch for this petticoat!" Charlotte screamed at Amber. "It's not stiff enough for the Ball!"

"More lace for my cuffs. More powder for my wig!" Louisa bellowed.

It was less than an hour since Amber had returned, and already the Uglies were tormenting her.

"Lazy creature, bring me my fan!" Louisa ranted.

"Mother, Cinderella has ruined my best petticoat!" Charlotte whined.

Octavia stormed from room to room. She ran at Amber and pinched her arm until it was black and blue. "I'll teach you to run away, ungrateful child! Just wait until after the Ball, when I have time to deal with you."

So nothing's changed, Amber thought, rubbing her sore arm. And she remembered Buttons' warnings about

Octavia and her three dead husbands.

"Mo-ther!" Charlotte screamed again. "Tell Cinderella to wash my petticoat with more starch, or else I'll pull her hair out, so there!"

It was late at night and the house was dark.

Amber was in the kitchen, starching and ironing Charlotte's petticoat until it stood up by itself.

I did the right thing, she reminded herself. *OK, so I walked back into a shrieking madhouse, but I couldn't stay away – not after what Tom told Buttons!*

Tomorrow was Saturday, the day of the Prince's Ball. Amber's arms ached, her hands and heart were sore.

At last she ironed the final crease out of the stiff petticoat.

She picked it up and shook it straight. "Where's a girl's fairy godmother when she needs her?" she grumbled out loud.

"Cinderella!" Louisa roared from the top of the cellar steps. "I want you in my room at once!"

"Coming!" Amber replied. *Yeah, fairy godmother*, Amber-Cinderella thought as she trudged up the stairs. *Isn't it time you showed up with your magic wand?*

10

"I can't sleep," Charlotte complained when Amber reached her bedside. "I'm so excited about the Ball tomorrow."

Is that why you dragged me up here – to tell me that? Amber thought.

Charlotte tossed and turned in her bed. "Of course, you'll miss all the fun, Cinderella. The Prince only invites important people to the Palace – not grubby kitchen workers like you."

Yeah, rub my nose in it, why don't you?
Amber thought with a frown.

"Mother says you should count yourself
lucky that you have a roof over your head
at all," Charlotte taunted, peering out
from under the covers with a smirk. "For
two pins she would turn you out into the
street as a common beggar!"

Amber took a deep breath. "May I go
now?" she asked quietly.

"Yes, nuisance – go!" Charlotte rolled
over and turned her back. "After all, I
need my beauty sleep for the Ball
tomorrow night!"

Amber slipped away from Charlotte's
bedside. She tiptoed along the gallery,

past Louisa's room and on towards Octavia's open door.

"This must be done in the dead of night," Octavia said to a man in a long black cloak. "No one must know!"

The man had his back to the door. He nodded.

"We must be rid of Cinderella once and

for all," Octavia went on.

Amber froze.

"The old man dotes on her and intends to leave her all his money when he dies," Octavia explained to the mystery visitor.

Outside the room, Amber's heart beat fast. Was this how pitiless Octavia had got rid of her three husbands, she wondered.

"I have tried my best to work Cinderella to death, to no avail," Octavia went on. "Then I thought I might poison her, but that is so easily found out."

The man muttered under his breath.

She seriously plans to bump me off! Amber thought.

"That is why I need you," Octavia said to the man. "Tonight you will kidnap her and take her out of the city to the forest on the mountain. You will leave her there, alone with no way out."

Buttons was right! She's a nasty, evil, horrid woman!

"Tonight, then," the man muttered.

"On the stroke of midnight!" Octavia agreed.

Yeah, and I won't be around to watch it happen! Amber promised herself, holding her breath and creeping on down the corridor.

Down in the cellar, Amber shook with fear.

This was serious – she only had a few hours to find a way out of this nightmare!

"I'm freezing!" she said out loud, hugging herself and creeping nearer still to the embers of the dying fire.

But even though the fire warmed her, Amber still trembled. She felt so gloomy and afraid that she began to cry.

What am I going to do? she asked herself, trying but failing to hold back the tears. *I suppose I could tell the old man about Octavia's kidnap plan, but he'd never believe me. She would deny it, and he's totally under her thumb.*

"I guess I could run away again," she muttered out loud, reaching for a poker and gently stirring the glowing embers. "I could find Buttons' house and hide from the spooky kidnapper!"

Suddenly, as she raked through the coals, red sparks flew from the fire. They rose from the grate and blew into the cellar, dancing in the dark.

Amber jumped back. The sparks floated round her head and filled the room. Then, in a burst of fiery orange light, a figure appeared.

"Hello, Cinderella," the fairy godmother said to her.

About time too! Amber thought.

The fairy waved her wand and the sparks died, leaving her surrounded by a soft silver glow. "Do not be unhappy, my child. Dry your tears, for you *shall* go to the Ball!"

Amber staggered back from the good fairy. "No, listen!" she pleaded. "I'm not crying because I'm – sad – about the Ball!"

The fairy godmother interrupted. She was dainty and pretty, and twinkled with silver light as she spoke. "You will wear the most beautiful pink satin gown," she promised. "You will go to the palace in a golden coach pulled by six white horses."

"I don't want to go to the Ball!" Amber insisted.

"First, we must give you your gown," the

fairy went on busily. She tiptoed round Amber like a ballerina. "Let's see. Shall it be trimmed with pale pink bows? How many petticoats shall you wear?"

"You're not listening!" Amber cried. "I don't care about the dress. I don't care about the Prince or the party! All I want is to get out of here!"

"Ttt-tt-tt!" The fairy clicked her tongue. "Pale pink ribbon will suit you," she decided.

Amber shook her head. "I know you think I'm Cinderella, but I'm not," she tried to explain. "I'm just plain, ordinary Amber who got here by mistake!"

"Consider, my dear." The fairy godmother waved her wand at Amber. "Your gown will make you the most

beautiful girl at the Ball. The Prince will look at no one but you!"

"Help!" Amber sighed, gazing down at her ragged red skirt and wishing with all her heart that she'd never taken it from her dressing-up box and put it on.

The fairy waved her wand again. "Stand still, Cinderella!"

Amber glanced up and felt the silver light surround her. When she looked down again, she saw that she was dressed in a wonderful gown of pink satin, trimmed with dainty pale pink bows.

"Fit for a princess!" the fairy godmother said with a satisfied smile.

The gown was beautiful, Amber had to admit. The skirt was full and flowing. Glowing pearls were sewn into the bodice, the cuffs were fringed with finest white lace.

"Oh!" Amber gasped. She had never in her life seen a dress so gorgeous. And she, Amber, was wearing it, walking around the dark kitchen, hearing it swish as she stepped.

"Turn around," the fairy instructed,

happy with her magical handiwork. "Let me see how the skirt flares out as you dance."

So Amber turned. And turned.

And in an instant she was surrounded by a gold and silver glitter that lit up the cellar and dazzled her as she twirled.

With eyes closed, Amber turned until she grew dizzy.

"Amber?" Lily gasped.

Amber rubbed her eyes and opened them. She saw her friend standing by the dressing-up box. It was daylight. The sun streamed through the basement door.

Lily dashed forward. "Amber, where have you been? We've been looking everywhere for you. Where did you get that dress?"

Amber looked down at the shiny, smooth satin.

"Wow, I mean, Amber . . . Wow!" Lily was speechless.

Just then, Pearl came running downstairs. "Amber's mum's losing it," she warned Lily. "She says that if Amber doesn't come up for tea right now, she's going to give her pizza to the dog! . . . Wow!"

Pearl stopped the moment she saw Amber in her pink satin dress. "Where did you get that?" she demanded.

"I – er – I . . ." For a moment Amber wanted to explain to Pearl and Lily exactly what had happened.

No, they'll never believe it, she thought. *Not in a million years!* So she changed her mind.

"I got it from the dressing-up box," she said with a broad grin. "Come on, I'll race you upstairs!"

A sneak peek at Amber's next adventure:

The Diamond Tiara

1

"Girls, what did you do with my old gardening hat?" Amber's mum asked.

Lily, Pearl and Amber were watching TV.

"We took it down to the dressing-up box in the basement like you told us," Pearl replied.

"Did I really tell you to do that?" Amber's mum couldn't remember. "Well, I need it after all. Amber, can you fetch it from the dressing-up box for me?"

"Later?" Amber pleaded. She wanted to watch her programme.

Her mum was ready to go out and garden. She stood in front of the telly. "Now," she said.

The three girls ran down to the basement and threw back the lid of Amber's dressing-up box.

"It's stuffed to the brim!" Lily exclaimed.

"Old shoes and boots, skirts, dresses, shawls . . .!" Pearl sighed.

"I know. It'll take ages to find Mum's hat," Amber grumbled.

"This is cool." Pearl picked out a cotton dress with zingy lemon stripes.

"Mum wore it to the beach when I was

two." Amber recognised it from the family photo album. "But hey, we're supposed to be looking for her gardening hat."

"I like this." Lily dipped into the box and picked out a shiny red shawl with a long fringe. She wrapped it round her shoulders.

"Hat!" Amber reminded them. At this rate they'd never catch the end of their TV programme.

Pearl dipped into the big box and held up a pink wedding hat with wonky feathers. "Is it this one?"

"Nope." Amber looked again. She pulled out a straw hat with a black band. It was crushed out of shape. "No, this was Dad's," she muttered.

"Let me try it!" Lily giggled as

she jammed it on her head.

"Do I suit this pink?" Pearl asked, trying on the wedding hat. She did a catwalk strut across the room.

Amber frowned and dug deep into the box. She chucked out one silver high-heeled shoe, a bent fairy wand and a long silk scarf.

Lily grabbed the wand. "Where are the wings?" she demanded. "There are fairy wings in here somewhere!"

"Hat!" Amber said crossly. It was no good – she would have to jump in the box and rummage in the bottom. She found the other silver shoe and a single white leather glove.

"Da-dah!" Pearl cried, leaning in and seizing a wide-brimmed cowboy hat. She chucked the wedding hat back into the box.

"Hey, cool!" Lily found what she had been looking for and strapped on some glittery wings.

Buried chin-deep in dressing-up clothes, Amber searched for her mum's gardening hat. She dragged an object to the surface – a dusty straw bonnet with a grubby white ribbon. *Is this it?* she wondered. And she tried it on.

"Ha-ha!" Fairy Lily laughed when she saw Amber in the old bonnet.

"No way would your mum wear that," Cowboy Pearl said.

Amber tried to take the hat off but something weird was happening. The hat was jammed on her head, she was

slipping down under the dressing-up clothes, amongst the silks, satins and sequins. And she could see a bright light at the bottom of the box.

"Amber, where are you?" Pearl ran to the box and peered in. A silver light shone. A cloud of golden glitter rose into the air.

Have you checked out...

www.dressingupdreams.net

It's the place to go for games, downloads, activities, sneak previews and lots of fun!

You'll find a special dressing-up game and lots of activities and fun things to do, as well as news on Dressing-Up Dreams and all your favourite characters.

Sign up to the newsletter at **www.dressingupdreams.net** to receive extra clothes for your Dressing-Up Dreams doll and the opportunity to enter special members only competitions.

What happens next...?
Log onto www.dressingupdreams.net for a sneak preview of my next adventure!

WIN A Dressing-Up Dreams GOODIE BAG!

CAN YOU SPOT THE TWO DIFFERENCES AND THE HIDDEN LETTER IN THESE TWO PICTURES OF AMBER?

There is a spot-the-difference picture and hidden letter in the back of all four Dressing-Up Dreams books about Amber (look for the books with 1 to 4 on the spine). Hidden in one of the pictures above is a secret letter. Find all four letters and put them together to make a special Dressing-Up Dreams word, then send it to us. Each month, we will put the correct entries in a draw and one lucky winner will receive a magical Dressing-Up Dreams goodie bag including an exclusive Dressing-Up Dreams keyring!

Send your magical word, your name and your address
on a postcard to: **The Dressing-Up Dreams Competition**

COLOURING FUN!

Carefully colour the Dressing-Up Dreams picture on the next page and then send it in to us.

Or you can draw your very own fairytale character. You might want to think about what they would wear or if they have special powers.

Each month, we will put the best entries on the website gallery and one lucky winner will receive a magical Dressing-Up Dreams goodie bag!

Send your drawing, your name and your address on a postcard to:
The Dressing-Up Dreams Competition

UK Readers:
Hodder Children's Books
338 Euston Road
London NW1 3BH
kidsmarketing@hodder.co.uk

Australian Readers:
Hachette Children's Books
Level 17/207 Kent Street
Sydney NSW 2000
childrens.books@hachette.com.au

New Zealand Readers:
Hachette Livre NZ Ltd
PO Box 100 749
North Shore City 0745
childrensbooks@hachette.co.nz